The Heart Of It

Andrea Manno

A Dream

Land of abundance, many fields

Dogs roaming around, feeling free

I have a dream of saving them

I think they'll be saving me

A house of shipping containers

Decked out in a homely way

Old buses converted into cabins

Where people can come and stay

I have a dream of saving dogs

The ones that are on death row

The many lives that I could save

I want to realise it, that I know

I need to develop a business model

One that will actually sustain

The saving of the dogs in need

There is so much love to gain

Australia 2018

The voice sounds out to media

A puppet steered from those

Behind the curtains

Where they cannot be seen

The voice sounds out to media

What they mean who really knows

We can never be certain

What they truly do mean

Changes all the time

A new PM, a high turnover

The conservatives are scary

Who will look after the Earth?

Their politics are not mine

They make me feel so sober

About what could possibly be

What is humanity really worth?

They change policies constantly
We need to really care more
About the reality of conservation
And helping the Labourforce
The massive growth of technology
Topics of health are so sore
As the conservatives' motivation
Is not as invested with resources

We should be clever and conscious
Of physical and mental health
Of providing for the people
The job market is in strife
We should be clever and conscious
Of spreading out the wealth
Letting everyone climb a steeple
To look after the issues so rife

The National Disability scheme
A worthy cause to be utilised
Investment into public schools
Making the corporates pay more tax
Things are not always as they seem
Politicians so often criticised
Swirling words around in pools
Of lies and promises not in tact

Let's see what we can achieve
Rallying against the fracking
Mining companies allowed to reap
Drilling into our precious ground

They are corporate thieves

It's important to keep tracking

And rally against, take a leap

Bring about voices, strong sound

We can do this if we believe

Strongly invested and fighting

To make the world a better place

And wish for a change in motion

We can do this and achieve

Changes through our fighting

Value humanity and shared space

Inspired by inner spirit potion

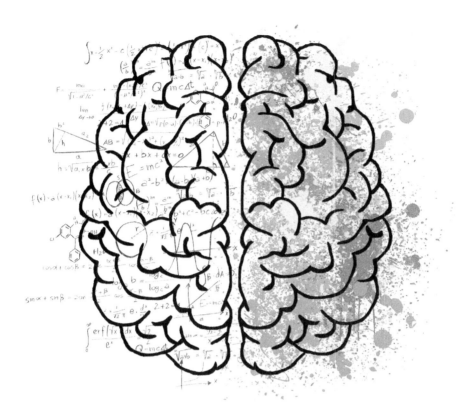

Change

The sun opened up the day

And encouraged me out to play

The spark of light ignites

Inspiring me to see the sights

I might take a short walk

And give myself positive talk

Footsteps, one by one along

In my head, my own life song

Thoughts tumbling in my head

I need to focus on senses instead

Wondering what it all means

But all is not what it seems

What could I say to change

Why I feel so darn strange?

The walls are far too thin

But I can push past to win

The sun could come out to stay

And make it a more pleasant day

And I too will start to shine

It only takes a bit of time

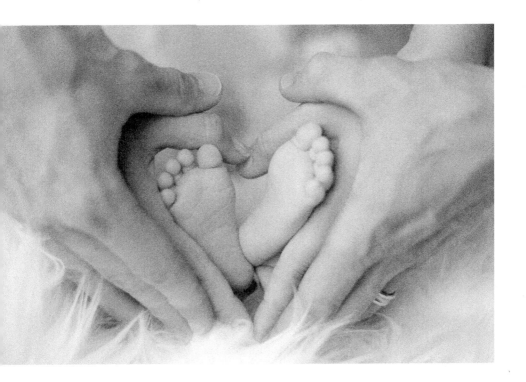

Dear Mum

A woman stands before me

The spirit is filled

With the magical energy

I'm proud, she's my Mum

Through thick and thin

Life's journey of roads

Together, we always win

Because we are bonded

A woman of utter strength

To carry me into life

She will go to any length

To protect and shelter

Of this woman, I'm so proud

She inspires me to live

A life where I can be loud

And happy to be who I am

I am grateful for her presence

I am thankful for all she is

And has done giving all essence

Of a mother's pure love for me

For A Mum

painting on the wall

ook upon it fondly

om within, there's a call

And I know that very voice

I hear it so close by

It's my mother with love

I utterly cherish the tie

That we have between us

A painting on the wall

The work of my mother

Spreading the love tall

Ever growing and never-ending

She has been an utter rock

Throughout my entire life

My mother can unlock

The life breathing in me

I feel such gratefulness

For the love we cherish

The pure heart of kindness

That my mother gives me

I look upon the painting

And feel her energy

It is so transpiring

Giving me such strength

It's almost beyond me

To put in words what she means

To me and what I can see

In her beautiful soul

The painting on the wall

That's her work with love

And from it she calls

With pure motherly love

Fortune

The lucky bamboo grows

It brings good fortune

What will be, who knows

But I watch it's growth

In abundance is foliage

Pleasure-seeking for me

From sitting on the ledge

And unwilling to jump

The twists in the stem

The walking of my path

It is a true lucky gem

Maybe that's for me

Touching the delicate leaves

Feeling the texture

Wondering how it achieves

Such beauty that I see

Haiku Attempts

Happiness is blissful

When you are true to yourself

And that is soul

The gardens grow well

When the plants are tended to

That is surely growth

Love is pure and gold

When it is true and fulfilling

And that is lovely

One's personality is gold

When truth is told and is pure

To make one's self true

map of the mind

has many lines drawn within

his is part of me

Her

From the moment I saw her

I knew that there was something

Nothing could make me deter

From getting to know this woman

She is a rose among the thorns

A gentle set of waves flowing

Together we could battle storms

And we as an "us" could be glowing

We have an expanse of sky

To learn about one another

No one may understand why

How we know to be together

Walk together in growth

There's learning for both

Ingliano

La musica of our languages in tongue,

The rhythm of yours so moving, hear!

Communication, it can be so unclear;

To articulate by the Italiano beat

The soul that inflames with such heat

Into expressions that can be sung!

There is a world between you and me

We can build a bridge for paths to cross-

For the space without you feels like loss

If we simply open our eyes and see!

La luna signals when the sun will fade,

The clock-hand ticks but not the same

Over space in which we lose and gain.

Cards on the table; who shall fold?

Let us decipher by symbols of old-

Heat and cool of our language made.

L'Inglese morphology of less inflection

The English pitch is my native to offer,

Requite with alternate meaning, you proffer-

By compromise and with effort, we serve

A mutual meeting upon our exchange curve:

Guiding acceptance without perfection.

There is a world between you and me

We can build a bridge for paths to cross-

For the space without you feels like loss

If we simply open our eyes and see!

Oceano of currents with ardent tremor!

Messages hanging off branches in sway

Letters that gather in rhetoric to say:

But for the semantics, we could interchange,

The hurdles so grande have since waned;

Let us now move in tune: new tenor!

There is a world between you and me

We can build a bridge for paths to cross-

For the space without you feels like loss

If we simply open our eyes and see!

Lament

The foliage grows in abundance

It's beautiful, nature's green

It's beauty is in its essence

And it is amazing to be seen

Yet here I sit and lament

Upon the leaves that have fallen

There's so much time I have spent

I feel so often crestfallen

Roses could brighten my day

Stalling to breathe in their scent

I think of many words to say

About beauty that nature has sent

The garden provides many delights

And I can take in pleasant sights

Love Sewn

The roses are out in bloom

The beauty that is sewn

Together we can be soon

And call our love our own

The soil we stand upon

Feeling our bare feet in it

Birds singing out our song

And in harmony we can sit

We watch the world go by

The animals in their glee

We let out a relaxed sigh

And enjoy what we can be

Patterns

The warmth of the glow

Sunshine filtering through

Wondering what we know

And writing things anew

The growth of the trees

All the pieces of life

The green foliage of leaves

The memories that are rife

The patterns of environment

The cycle that takes place

Nature's way of sentiment

Among it, finding own space

The growing tree of life's lore

Spreading wings to make me soar

Saving Dogs

Land of abundance, many fields

Dogs roaming around, feeling free

I have a dream of saving them

I think they'll be saving me

A house of shipping containers

Decked out in a homely way

Old buses converted into cabins

Where people can come and stay

I have a dream of saving dogs

The ones that are on death row

The many lives that I could save

I want to realise it, that I know

I need to develop a business model

One that will actually sustain

The saving of the dogs in need

There is so much love to gain

The Human Connection

ook into her eyes

ney tell no lies

ne has a unique beauty

nd a wonderful personality

ne is like a flower

med with inner power

ould drown in her love

Spread my wings like a dove

I could bask in her glow

And let us follow our flow

Allow this emotional connection

And enjoy one another's affection

What will be will just be

And with her I can be just me

Walking the Earth

Turning the Earth around

While my mind goes round

Like a washing machine

Thinking how I might seem

Looking inwards to myself

Finding the truth of self

For me there is a place

Finding my very own space

My existence is unique

My interests are at peak

Back to finding motivation

Bringing back my inspiration

Turning the Earth around

While my mind goes round

Like a washing machine

Thinking how I might seem

Who am I in this life?

One who seeks a wife

To walk the land together

To brave all the weather

I will continue to write

And fly it like a kite

Soaring up and moving forward

It's time to go onward

Wandering and Wondering

Walking with the crunching

Below my sneakers

Feeling the dirt beneath

Among other seekers

Of Earth's offering

While gently pondering

The spirit at the core

Feeling dizzy

Smelling the diverse scents

Keeping mind busy

Traipsing around and along

Armed with an inner song

What will be will be

Allowing the time

The skies over me blue

Thinking what is mine

Stop and smell the scents

Allow me time to ascent

Who Am I?

ootsteps slowly and with uncertainty

aking it moment by moment, each day

n searching to find what is me

ho I am, finding my own true way

wo steps forward, ten go backwards

seems like I'm battling myself

eed to ensure that I move onwards

And keep travelling, growth of self

If I turn abruptly and lose my way

I live experiences and learn from them

My unique path upon which I sway

Back and forth but back to the stem

I need to approach myself with understanding

And allow some bit of self-compassion

Fight the issues that are longstanding

And follow my heart, my inner passion

It is how I will find my own true way

By following my goals and even my dreams

To live in the present, day by day

And realise that I can make my themes

Why Candy?

The aisles of colour that beckon me,
tantalising, teasing, drawing my eyes
to the endless possibilities, seemingly
offered up, each one that I spy.

Among the rows and stacks to be
options considered for me to buy,
so many products - a shopping spree!
The big question really is 'why?'

They're all good for us, they decree,
things upon which we must rely-
at least, that's what they want us to see
and yet it seems to be a big web of lies.

What is it that is good for me

under these vast skies?

So many possibilities, each for a fee

but it's much better if you cut the ties.

You

I see your face in glee

And your kind eyes to me

When I look upon you

I know we can get through

The sun rays shine down

To wipe away any frown

We can spend a happy time

And I think of you as mine

Our garden can constantly grow

As we weave what we can sew

New sprouts that keep growing

Allowing what is naturally flowing

Sometimes there are cloudy days

But we can get through in our ways

And continue to get to know

One another, together we grow

Printed in Great Britain
by Amazon

40291168R00030